Monster Boy

To

Ralph

Cover design and page layout by Circus Design

Library of Congress Cataloging-in-Publication Data

Winn, Christine M.
      Monster boy / by Christine M. Winn, with David Walsh ; illustrated by Christine M. Winn.
            p.   cm.
      Summary: Hotheaded Buster has trouble making friends, but he learns a valuable lesson when a meets a monster in the woods on the way to school.
      ISBN 0-925190-87-X (acid-free)
      [1. Anger—Fiction.   2. Monsters—Fiction.   3. Schools—Fiction.]   I. Walsh, David.   II. Title.
PZ7.W72974Mo   1996
[Fic]—dc20   95-43558
                                                                         CIP
                                                                         AC

First Printing: March 1996
Printed in the United States of America

00 99 98 97 96   7 6 5 4 3 2 1

Published by Fairview Press, 2450 Riverside Avenue South, Minneapolis, MN 55454.

For a current catalog of Fairview Press titles, please call this Toll-Free number: 1-800-544-8207

Publisher's Note: Fairview Press publishes books and other materials related to the subjects of physical health, mental health, chemical dependency, and other family issues. Its publications, *including Monster Boy,* do not necessarily reflect the philosophy of Fairview Hospital and Healthcare Services or their treatment programs.

The paper used in this publication meets the minimum requirements of American National Standard for Information Sciences—Permanence of Paper for Printed Library Materials, ANSI Z329.48-1984.

Monster Boy

by

Christine M. Winn
with David Walsh, Ph.D.

Illustrated by Christine M. Winn

Fairview Press

Fairview Press
Minneapolis, Minnesota

"Buster looks like he's eating worms," joked Jake.

"Oh, yeah? Well, you're a stupid noodle head!" yelled Buster, and he dumped his plate of spaghetti on Jake's head.

Jake had forgotten the number one rule of Wooddale Elementary School. Don't make Buster angry.

That was the beginning of a very bad week for Buster. On Tuesday, he called his teacher a toad-kissing peanut brain for giving him a low grade in history. On Wednesday, he struck out in the big game and picked a fight with *both* baseball teams.

By the next day, Buster had forgotten the fight and wanted to play baseball.

"Hey, guys, throw the ball here!" called Buster.

"No way!" replied Jake. "We don't want to play with a bully."

Buster slapped the ball out of Jake's hands. "Well, who wants to play with a bunch of babies anyway!" he yelled. But Buster did want to play with them. He wanted the boys to be his friends.

"Why doesn't any one like me?" Buster asked his mom that night.

"Buster, you have to learn to tame your outbursts," she answered. "We've talked about this time after time. When you get angry, you lash out at people in a scary way. You frighten people. You don't want that, do you?

Buster rolled his eyes, just like he did every time his mother lectured him about his temper. Then he made a silly face and stomped monster-like around the living room. "Ga-rowl! Raar! Better run and hide! Here I come!" mocked Buster.

Buster's mom just shook her head. "You're going to have to learn the hard way," she said quietly.

The next morning Buster's mom overslept.
"Buster, I'm sorry I didn't get you up on time.
You'll have to hurry or you'll be late for school,"
she said as she pushed Buster out the door.

Buster decided to take what he thought was a
shortcut through the forest. Far into the forest
and too late to turn back Buster realized his
"shortcut" was actually too long. "This stinks!"
griped Buster. "Crud! Double crud! Now I'm
really going to be late."

Buster was so angry he picked up rocks
and pitched them at the trees. "Take that,
stupid forest! You stinky old trees! Shortcut—
BALONEY!" he screamed. One rock after
another crashed into the trunks of the trees
and chipped off bits of bark. Then one of the
rocks missed the trees and went flying into the
dark—until it hit something with a thud. Buster
heard a huge growl. Maybe he'd hit a bear!

The growl became louder and meaner
as something pushed through the trees toward
Buster. Suddenly Buster was face-to-face with
a foul-smelling monster, much bigger,
much scarier, and much uglier than a bear.
The monster roared so hard it blew Buster's hat
right off his head.

"R A A A R !"

Buster was still so angry about the shortcut that he didn't stop to think twice. "Get lost, you overgrown hairball. You dog-breath, dork-head, fleabag!" Then with everything Buster had inside him, he growled back at the monster. "GA-ROWL!"

Buster didn't frighten the creature at all. So he roared again, this time meaner and louder. The monster just stamped its feet and swung its great claws in the air and screamed at Buster. And Buster did the same.

Without knowing it, Buster was changing.
With every angry growl, scream, and stomp,
Buster was turning into a monster.

Buster and the monster started to hit and punch. They tumbled across the floor of the forest until they fell into the river. As Buster picked himself up out of the water, he happened to see his scary reflection.

"Agh!" he yelled. "Is that me? Have I turned into a monster?" Buster turned around and saw the other monster rolling on the ground laughing.

"How did this happen? Why? WHY?" cried Buster.

"You act like a monster, you become a monster," the creature said with a huge snort.

Buster looked back at his image in the water. "I don't want to be a monster!" cried Buster. "People are scared of monsters. I just want to be a boy. I want people to like me."

"Monster boy! Monster boy!" mocked the creature. "No one likes a monster boy!"

"Stop it!" yelled Buster. "I'm not going to be a monster anymore." He turned and started walking away.

"Monster boy! Monster boy!" laughed the creature. "No one likes a monster boy!"

The monster's teasing made Buster angry again. He wanted to scream back at the monster. Instead he took a deep breath and kept walking away.

When Buster didn't hear the monster call out any more, he peeked over his shoulder. The monster was still sitting where Buster left him, only the creature didn't look scary any more. He looked sad and lonely.

As Buster walked on to school, he worried about being a monster boy. He knew he'd have to change the monster inside him if he ever hoped to make friends.

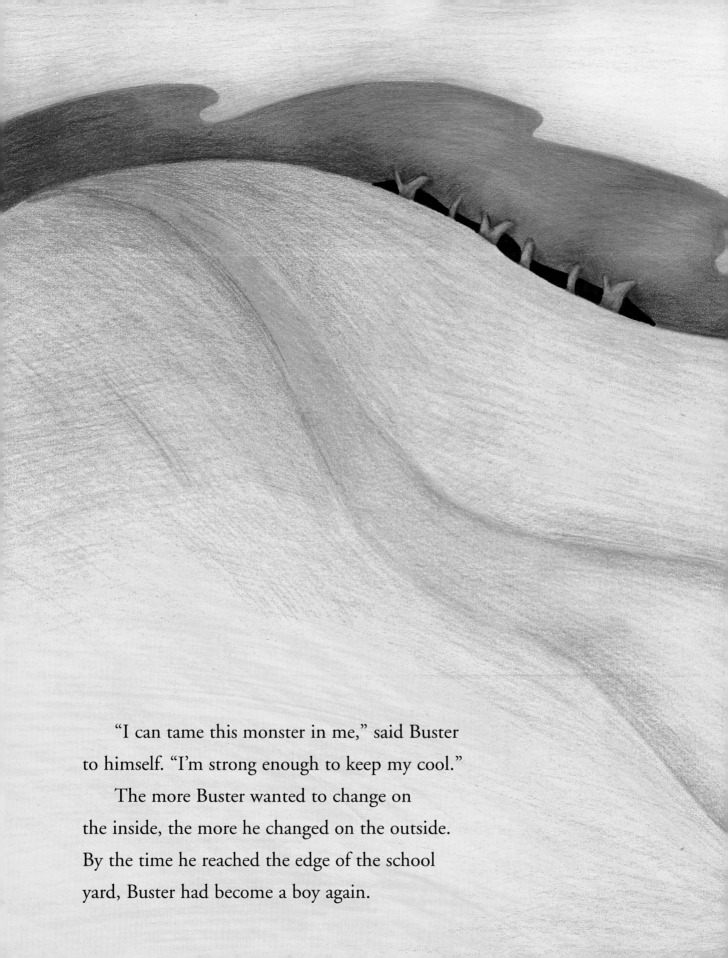

"I can tame this monster in me," said Buster
to himself. "I'm strong enough to keep my cool."
   The more Buster wanted to change on
the inside, the more he changed on the outside.
By the time he reached the edge of the school
yard, Buster had become a boy again.

Buster wasn't late for school after all. The children were still in the yard playing. Jake and the guys were about to start a baseball game.

Buster walked up to them. "I'm sorry I've been a jerk," he said. "I'm really sorry." Then he continued walking toward the school.

Jake and the boys looked at each other in surprise. They had never heard Buster say he was sorry about anything.

"Hey, Buster! You want to play third base or shortstop?" Jake called out.

"I like shortstop, if that's okay!" answered Buster.

Other children's books by Fairview Press:

Alligator in the Basement, by Bob Keeshan, TV's Captain Kangaroo
illustrated by Kyle Corkum

Box-Head Boy, by Christine M. Winn with David Walsh, Ph.D.
illustrated by Christine M. Winn

Clover's Secret, by Christine M. Winn with David Walsh, Ph.D.
illustrated by Christine M. Winn

My Dad Has HIV, by Earl Alexander, Sheila Rudin, Pam Sejkora
illustrated by Ronnie Walter Shipman